Worry Warriors is published by Stone Arch Books,
A Capstone Imprint
1710 Roe Crest Drive
North Mankato, Minnesota 56003
www.mycapstone.com

Library of Congress Cataloging-in-Publication Data
Names: Ventura, Marne, author.
Title: Jittery Jake conquers stage fright / by Marne Ventura.
Description: North Mankato, Minnesota: Stone Arch Books, a Capstone imprint, [2017]
I Series: Worry warriors I Summary: When he is assigned the part of King Midas in the
third grade play, Jake Williams is worried because he really does not like performing
in front of others—but the Worry Warriors, the club he and his three best friends
formed, are there to help him overcome his stage fright.
Identifiers: LCCN 2016016968I ISBN 9781496536129 (library binding) I ISBN
9781496536518 (paperback) I ISBN 9781496536556 (ebook pdf) Subjects: LCSH:
Stage fright—Juvenile fiction. I Anxiety—Juvenile fiction. I Children's plays—Juvenile
fiction. I Elementary schools—Juvenile fiction. I Best friends—Juvenile fiction. I CYAC:
Stage fright—Fiction. I Worry—Fiction. I Plays—Fiction. I Schools—Fiction. I Best friends—
Fiction. I Friendship—Fiction.Classification: LCC PZ7.1.V445 Ji 2017 I DDC 813.6 [Fic] —dc23
LC record available at https://lccn.loc.gov/2016016968

Editor: Michelle Bisson
Designer: Hilary Wacholz

Printed in Canada.
009643F16

Worry WARRIORS

Jittery Jake Conquers Stage Fright

by Marne Ventura
illustrated by Leo Trinidad

STONE ARCH BOOKS
a capstone imprint

TABLE OF CONTENTS

Worry WARRIORS

My name is Jake Williams. I live with my mother and sister in a city near the beach in California. My dad and mom split up before I was born, so it's always been just the three of us. I'm nine years old. Sometimes Mom calls me Little Neil. That's because I have curly black hair and dark brown skin like the famous astrophysicist Neil deGrasse Tyson. Also because I want to be a scientist someday. One awesome thing about my neighborhood is that my three best friends live on my block. Adam, Nellie, Estella, and I have known each other since preschool.

Estella is an expert on movies and TV shows. She knows the names of all the actors, especially the kids. She loves dancing and cheerleading. She also likes hanging out with her family.

Nellie likes reading, writing, word games, and school. That's excellent because she wants to be a writer when she grows up.

Adam is awesome at sports, art, and building projects. He has dyslexia. That means he learns to read, write, and spell differently than most kids.

Three summers ago, when we were six, we were making hula-hoop bubbles in Nellie's backyard. We were barefoot, running around on the wet grass. Estella almost stepped on a bee. She freaked out. She ran onto Nellie's back porch and wouldn't budge until Adam scooped up the bee with a plastic cup and put it into the trash can.

Then Estella said she felt silly, being scared of teeny bees. But that she felt better after she told us and we didn't laugh at her.

I guess Nellie didn't want Estella to feel silly alone, because she told us that she was afraid of the dark

at bedtime. She imagined scary stuff, like that her toys might come to life and attack her, or that coyotes might be hiding in her closet.

Then Adam said he got scared walking across the bridge over the freeway. He held onto his mom's hand and didn't look down.

So I told my friends my own babyish secret. I was afraid to wade into the ocean because I could feel slimy stuff with my feet. What if I stepped on a poison jellyfish?

After we told each other our worries, we felt better. We didn't make fun of each other the way some kids would. And, if all of us had secret worries, maybe they weren't silly at all.

That's when Nellie had a great idea. She said we should form a club. First we would tell each other our worries. Then together we would fight them, like knights and warrior princesses in shining armor.

And that's how we became the Worry Warriors.

Chapter 1

Winter Extravaganza

It's a Monday afternoon in late November. I'm sitting at a table outside the Ocean View Elementary School cafeteria with Adam, Estella, and Nellie. We've just finished lunch. Winter break is three weeks away, but it's still warm and sunny. I watch a monarch butterfly glide across the courtyard. It drifts toward the eucalyptus trees at the edge of the playground.

"Dad said he'd walk with me downtown to The Bookworm after school," says Nellie. "A new book in my mystery series is out. You guys want to come?"

"I would, but I've got soccer practice," says Adam. He swings his feet under the bench.

"Sure," says Estella. "No dance class today."

"Okay," I say. "I just have to do a couple of chores first. I'm trying to earn enough money to buy a robot race car that I can control from my computer."

"Awesome," says Adam. "How do you control it?"

"You know that class Mom signed me up for last summer at the College-for-Kids program?" I say. "I learned to write computer programs that give directions. I can send the directions from the computer to the car, and it moves the way I tell it to!"

"How much is it?" asks Adam.

"$99.95," I reply. "I've just started saving. So far I have last week's allowance: nine dollars."

"Only $90.95 to go," Nellie says, smiling. "But don't forget shipping and handling. And tax."

"I didn't think of that," I say. "Maybe more than $90.95 to go. If tax is 8 percent, that will add eight dollars. And if shipping is 10 percent, that's another ten dollars."

"You are good at math!" Nellie says. "That's another eighteen dollars."

"I know," I say. "Two more weeks' allowance." I wonder how I'm ever going to save that much but keep that worry to myself.

The end-of-lunch-recess bell rings, and we head back to class. Estella, Adam, and I are in Ms. Anderson's fourth grade class. Nellie is next door in Mr. Meaney's. Before school started, she was nervous about getting a new teacher and about being in a different class than us. But he's nice, despite his name, and we still get to spend some time together at school.

After we line up, Ms. Anderson says, "We're going back to the Multipurpose Room with Mr. Meaney's class. We'd like to talk to you about the fourth grade's part in the upcoming Winter Extravaganza."

Estella twirls around with her arms up and curved, ballerina-style. "Yippee," she says. "I hope it's a play."

"Oh, no!" Adam says. "I thought we were having finish-your-work time. I was going to finish my reading questions so I won't have homework after soccer."

"Not fair," I say. "This is our computer lab time."

Every year on the night before winter break, the upper graders put on a show in the Multipurpose Room. Everyone's family comes, and each grade goes onstage for 20 minutes. Last year we made snowflakes to decorate the backdrop. We wore scarves and mittens and sang songs about winter.

It wasn't too bad. I'd never want to be an actor or a singer, but since the whole class was doing the same thing, it was okay. Still, I wouldn't mind skipping it. Especially if it means we have to miss our computer lab time because we have to practice.

When we get to the Multipurpose Room, we sit down at the lunch tables. There's a whiteboard on an easel in front of the stage.

"Tell us what you know about Greek mythology," says Ms. Anderson.

Nellie raises her hand. "The Greeks wrote stories to explain how Earth was created."

Mr. Meaney writes it on the whiteboard.

"What else?" asks Ms. Anderson. I raise my hand and she calls on me.

"They thought the world was flat like a paper plate," I say, "and that Greece was in the center. *So* not right." The kids laugh.

Brittany, the new girl in Nellie's class, raises her hand. "There were lots of gods and goddesses," she says. "Like Zeus and Athena."

Wow. Brittany is not just pretty. She's smart.

"Well done," says Ms. Anderson. "Words and themes from Greek mythology are still used today. Have you heard of the Midas touch?"

"That means you're good at making money," says Nellie.

"Right," says Mr. Meaney. "We're going to do a play about King Midas. He turned everything he touched into gold."

Ms. Anderson asks Brittany to hand out a stack of booklets. "These folders contain the myth and the play.

Your homework for tonight is to read them. Mr. Meaney and I have assigned your parts," Ms. Anderson says. "You'll find them on the last page."

Brittany hands me a folder. I look at her as I take it. Her eyes are amazingly blue. I guess I should be paying closer attention to my hand than her eyes, though, because the folder slides out before I can grab it. It lands on Brittany's foot. "Sorry," I say, as I lean over to get it.

At the same time, Brittany bends down to pick up the folder and we bump heads.

"Sorry," we both say.

I want to ask her if she's okay, but she moves away.

That was dumb. My face feels hot.

I push my glasses up and open my folder. I wonder what job I got? Usually I'm the one who turns the lights or the music on and off at the right time. I'd be okay with that.

But when I get to the cast and crew list, I can't believe what I see. Ms. Anderson gave me the part of King Midas.

Chapter 2

Robot Race Car

Nellie is waiting outside our classroom when Estella, Adam, and I come out. We always walk home together.

"What part did you get?" she asks.

"King Midas!" I put on my backpack. "Why would they choose *me* for the lead part?"

"You're smart," says Estella. "You have a good memory, and you are a great reader. I think it's awesome. I'm one of your three princess daughters. I'm so excited. I wonder what the costumes are like? I hope I get a long, sparkly dress."

"I hope I don't!" I blurt out. They all laugh and I blush.

"I know that didn't make sense," I say, "but I hate the

idea of getting up on stage in front of people. I was hoping to help backstage. Do you think I'll have to wear a costume?"

"Definitely." Estella smiles, like that's a good thing. "Probably a robe. And a crown, for sure."

"No way," I protest. "I'm not going onstage in front of everybody in a robe."

"I'm head set designer." Adam kicks a rock across the sidewalk. "I get to make the stage look like a castle. How cool is that?"

"I'm narrator," Nellie says quietly. "Narrator is a big part."

"You'll do great," I say. "It's me I'm worried about."

No one knows what to say, but by now we're in front of Nellie's house, so we just say goodbye.

I go home, find my key, open the door and go inside. Mom teaches eighth-grade math at Monarch Middle School, so we usually get home at the same time. If Mom's not here, I'm supposed to call her cell phone.

"Hi Jake!" she answers. "I got held up at a meeting. I should be home soon. Everything okay?"

"Yes," I say. "Can I go to The Bookworm with Nellie and Estella? Nellie's dad is going too."

"Okay," she says. "As long as you first check in on Mrs. Jensen."

Mrs. Jensen lives in the apartment building next to us. She was a teacher at Mom's school before she retired. She twisted her ankle last week, so she hired me to help her with chores until her ankle heals.

I eat an apple, lock my front door, get Mrs. Jensen's mail, and knock on her door.

She calls out, "Come on in, Jake."

Mrs. Jensen's white Scottie dog runs up and wags his tail. His whole back end wiggles.

"Hi, Magnus," I say. I give him a scratch behind the ears.

Mrs. Jensen's leg is propped up on a footrest. It's weird to see her sitting down. Usually she's riding her bike, jogging with Magnus, or working in the community garden.

"How's your ankle?" I ask as I hand her the mail.

"Getting better." She wiggles her foot. "A few more days and I'll be back to normal."

"Good! Is it okay if Magnus walks with us to The Bookworm?" I ask. "Nellie's dad is going too."

"Sure, if you don't mind staying outside with him while the others go in."

"That's fine. Need anything else?" I ask.

"Will you drop the envelopes from the kitchen table into the mailbox on your way?" she asks.

"Sure!" I reply, as I leash Magnus.

Magnus and I jog to Nellie's. Estella, Nellie, and Nellie's dad are waiting on the front porch.

Nellie's dad is really cool. He's a computer programmer. It's fun to talk to him about technology. He really gets the stuff that interests me.

As we walk, I tell him about the robot race car I'm saving up for.

"Sounds great," he says. "Can you control the speed as well as the direction?"

"Yes," I say. "It even has bluetooth, so you can run it wirelessly."

"Nice," says Nellie's dad. "Like a driverless car!"

"I figure it will take six more weeks to save enough," I say. "I get nine dollars allowance, and I can earn an extra ten dollars from Mom and Mrs. Jensen by walking Magnus and helping them both in the garden. But I can't spend money on anything else! It's going to be hard. Six weeks is a long time."

"It'll go by fast," says Nellie's dad. "You know what they say—time flies when you're having fun!"

***

We get to The Bookworm, and I sit down on the bench outside to wait with Magnus. The bookstore owners must like dogs, because there's a water dish by the door. Magnus laps up a drink. Then he sits and stares at me. His ears point up. The fur around his mouth is drippy. I think he's

smiling. I scratch his head and watch the people walk by. It's a good thing I'm staying outside. Whenever I go into The Bookworm, I find a book I want and buy it with my allowance money.

***

"I wanted a good part in the play," says Nellie as we walk home. She's got three new books tucked under one arm. "But now I feel super-nervous."

"I didn't even *want* a part," I tell her.

"It'll be fun." Estella twirls around a lamppost. "Nellie, what costume do you think the narrator will wear?"

"Oh, no!" Nellie shrieks. "I hadn't thought of that. Will I have to look like a Greek statue or something?" Nellie shifts her books to the other arm.

"Brittany and Ashley play my sisters," says Estella. "I wonder if we'll have matching gowns. And crowns?"

"Brittany's a princess?" I ask. This play is making me so anxious.

"The way I learned it, King Midas only had one daughter," says Nellie's dad.

"They added two for the play," says Nellie. "So more kids could have speaking parts."

"Makes sense. Too bad you can't build a robot to do your part, Jake," Nellie's dad says, winking at me. "Then you could control it from behind the scenes."

"I wish!" I say. His idea makes me smile, but also makes me more nervous. It also makes me wonder if I could build my own robot racecar for less money than the one I'm saving up for. But, I don't think I'm that good at electronics yet.

"We sing a song at the end," says Estella. "It's going to be so fun."

"Wait?! Who sings? " I ask. "Everyone sings? I am *not* singing by myself."

All this talk about the play gives me the jitters. I'd better get home and read it. I say goodbye, and Magnus and I jog back to Mrs. Jensen's.

"Thanks, Jake," she says when I return Magnus. "I don't know what I'd do without you."

She hands me a five-dollar bill.

"You don't need to pay me," I tell her. Mrs. Jensen is almost like a grandmother. I've known her ever since I can remember.

"I know," she says. "But I want to. And I'm sure you're saving up for something."

I tell her about my race car and she agrees that it sounds awesome.

$85.95 to go! Plus eighteen dollars for shipping, handling, and tax. It's going to be a long time before I get that car. Or have any spending money for other stuff. If Nellie's dad is right, and time flies when you're having fun, I guess I'm going to have to figure out how to have a lot of fun for free.

Chapter 3

King Midas

When I get home I hear Mom in the kitchen. "Yum!" I call, when I get a whiff of chili and cornbread. "I'm home!"

I go to my room and add my earnings to my money jar. I find a marker and write RACE CAR on both sides, to remind me not to spend any on other stuff. Then I grab my folder and take it out to the kitchen.

"How's it going, Jake?" Mom gives me a hug. "Do you have homework?"

"I have to read this play," I say. "Can you believe Ms. Anderson made me King Midas for the Winter Extravaganza?"

"Why, Jake, that's wonderful!" Mom gives me a kiss on the head.

"Wonderful? It's horrible." I open the folder and start to read. "Oh, no," I say, when I reach the end. "It's worse than I imagined. Look at all these lines I have to memorize."

I hand Mom the folder.

"And I think I have to wear a costume. I don't even like wearing costumes for Halloween."

"This is the lead part," says Mom as she reads. "Ms. Anderson clearly thinks you can do it."

"Maybe. But it means I'll miss computer lab time," I say. "And I wanted to earn extra money after school to buy a robot race car, not spend my time memorizing lines. It'll take forever!"

"You'll be great," Mom says. "Besides, myths are interesting. Ancient people who created myths were like Worry Warriors, in a way."

"What do you mean?"

"People can be frightened of things they don't understand," she explains. "Before science, they made up stories to explain nature. Like, why there's lightning."

"What does the myth of King Midas explain?" I ask.

"It's a different kind of myth," says Mom. "It explains human nature."

I'm about to ask Mom what that means when Amanda comes into the kitchen with her homework.

Amanda and Nellie's big sister, Lucy, are cheerleaders at Monarch Middle School. They must have had a rally today, because Amanda's wearing her blue and gray uniform, and a blue and gray bow in her curly ponytail. People say that Amanda looks like a mini-Mom. I'm not so sure. After all, mom wears eyeglasses, like me. Amanda can see perfectly without them.

Amanda sits down next to me at the kitchen table and sees my folder.

"Fourth grade Greek mythology play?" she asks.

I nod. "I have to be King Midas! I don't want to do it."

"We did Pandora's Box when I was in fourth grade. I wanted to be Pandora, but I had to turn the lights and music on and off backstage," she says sadly.

"That's what I wanted to do! Life is so unfair!" I say.

Amanda nods. "You can say that again."

"Why is life unfair for you?" I ask.

"Too much homework!," she exclaims. "Wait until you get to middle school, Jake. Instead of one teacher giving you assignments, you'll have six. Tonight I have math, English, and social studies."

"Want to help me practice my lines when you're done?" I ask Amanda. "And then play a video game?"

"By the time I'm done, it'll be bedtime," she says.

"That stinks," I say, but what I'm thinking again is: life is so unfair.

"Amanda," says Mom, "your turn to set the table."

Amanda heaves a sigh, then puts her homework aside and sets the table as Mom dishes up the food.

As we eat, I say, "Mom, do you think I could ask Ms. Anderson to give me a different job in the play? Like a backstage job?"

"I know you didn't choose to be King Midas," says Mom, "but it's an honor to be given the lead part. And doing things that are unfamiliar and challenging can be good for you."

Great. Just what I didn't want to hear. Mom is usually right, but … it still scares me.

"What were the costumes like when your class did the Greek mythology play?" I ask Amanda.

"Togas," she says. "And a crown of leaves. I was sad I didn't get to wear one."

"I don't want to wear a toga," I say. "What *is* a toga?"

"You know, those loose white dresses the Greeks wore," says Amanda. "With a gold belt, and sandals."

I eat a spoonful of chili and imagine being onstage in a dress.

"I feel sick," I say.

Mom puts her hand on my forehead.

"Not that kind of sick," I tell her, though I do kind of

feel like I want to throw up. "Sick, like, I don't want to be in the play."

"You should be happy," says Amanda. "You have the best part!"

"But what if I forget my lines?" I say. "What if I look silly in a toga? What if the other kids laugh at me?"

"I know just what you need," Amanda says, smiling at Mom.

Mom nods, puts one arm around my shoulder, and holds out the phone to Amanda with the other. "Let's give the phone to King Midas. He needs to set up an emergency Worry Warriors meeting."

Chapter 4

Emergency Meeting

The next day after school, Nellie, Adam, Estella, and I meet in Nellie's backyard clubhouse. That's where we always have our Worry Warriors meetings.

The clubhouse is really cool. Nellie's dad built it for Nellie's big brother, Henry, when he was little. Henry's starting high school this year, and he's on the track team, so he's pretty busy. He lets us use it any time we want.

We put on the Viking helmets that we got at the after-Halloween sale a couple of years ago. We know we're a bit old for this now, but it's tradition!

Then we raise our hands and yell, "Don't worry, be happy!" That's our Worry Warriors battle cry. It's how we always start meetings.

"I hereby call this meeting to order," says Nellie. "Let's start by saying what worries us about being in the school play."

We all settle into beanbag chairs.

"And remember," says Estella, "Nobody is allowed to say someone's worry is stupid."

"Right," says Adam. "What happens in the clubhouse, stays in the clubhouse."

"No making fun or laughing," I add.

"I'm excited about being narrator," says Nellie. "But I read the script last night, and I can't believe how many lines I have."

"Me too," I say. "And we can't read them. We have to know them by heart."

"That's show business," says Estella. "You have to memorize your lines."

"But you only have a few," I tell her. "Nellie and I have so many."

"I'm sure glad I get to paint the set," says Adam.

Estella flips through her folder. "You're right," she says. "Why don't I have more lines?"

"What happens if we forget our lines?" asks Nellie.

"Does Ms. Anderson think I can't handle a bigger part?" asks Estella.

"Will we get to use cue cards?" I ask. "I hope so."

"Ms. Anderson gave us directions for a toga costume," I tell Nellie. "Did Mr. Meaney give you the same thing?"

Nellie nods.

"It looks easy. They're going to give us the fabric," says Estella. "We just have to tie it on and pin it up the sides. And make a belt, and wear sandals."

"But it'll look stupid," I say. "It only goes over one shoulder. I don't want to wear a dress."

"You three seem to be getting more nervous," says Adam. "Maybe it's time for us to make a plan for fighting our worries. What can we do?"

"Go on strike?" I say.

"Leave a week early for winter break?" says Nellie. "We'll say we're visiting our grandparents."

"Be serious,"" says Estella. "Let's figure out how to do a good job. I want to show Ms. Anderson I'm ready for a bigger part in the next play."

"If we practice every day we can learn our lines," says Nellie. "We have to work at it."

"What about earning money for my race car?" I say. "And other homework? When am I going to find the time to learn lines?"

"We can practice when we're walking to school, and when we're on the playground," says Nellie. "That way you'll have time for other stuff after school."

"Good idea," says Estella.

"I'm going to ask about cue cards," I say.

Adam says, "Ms. Anderson taught me how to make this cool check-off chart. It helps me keep track of all the things I have to do. We can make one for you, Jake."

"I'll walk Magnus if you run out of time," says Estella.

"Wow, thanks, you guys," I say.

"I sort of feel better," says Nellie.

"I guess if I'm stuck being King Midas, I'd rather do a good job than goof it up." I say.

There's a knock on the clubhouse door, and Lucy sticks her head in. "Want to come and try a cupcake?"

"Meeting adjourned," Adam says.

We raise our arms and chant, "Don't worry, be happy!" before we head to the kitchen.

Adam's eyes get big when he sees the cupcakes on the kitchen table. "How many did you make?"

"We need three dozen for the fundraiser," says Amanda. "But we have extras." She hands one to Adam.

"Butterfly cupcakes," says Estella. "That's so cool. I want to be a cheerleader and bake cupcakes like this when I'm in sixth grade."

"Here, Nellie,"Amanda says. She hands her a cupcake.

There's a butterfly on top of the chocolate frosting. The wings are made from mini-pretzels, and the head is an orange M&M.

"They're so cute!" says Nellie.

"They taste good, too," says Adam, with a mouthful of cake.

I almost don't want to bite into my cupcake because it looks so cool. Amanda and I used to have fun baking stuff together. She's a genius at coming up with creative decorations. Sometimes it seems like Amanda's good at everything. It was fun having her for a big sister when we both went to the same school. I miss that.

"I hope we sell all of our cupcakes," says Lucy. "We're trying to raise enough for cheerleader camp."

"Speaking of money, I've got to go and see if Mrs. Jensen needs help," I say. "And walk Magnus. See you guys later."

As I jog to Mrs. Jensen's, I think about the Worry Warriors meeting. I feel less nervous about playing King Midas. But I sure have a lot of work to do.

Chapter 5

First Rehearsal

Our block has a community garden where both Mom and Mrs. Jensen grow vegetables. Mom pays me my allowance for doing chores at home. If I help her in the garden, I get extra pay. And Mrs. Jensen needs me to tend her garden until her ankle heals. She pays me too.

So, for the rest of the week, I'm pretty busy after school. First I check with Mrs. Jensen to see if she needs any errands done. Then I walk around the block a few times with Magnus.

Magnus is really smart. He knows to stop and wait at the crosswalk if there are cars going by. He's good on his leash unless he sees a squirrel. Then he goes crazy trying to chase it. He likes to dig holes, so if I take him with me when I work in the garden, I have to keep an eye on him. No one ever said walking a dog was easy.

Working in the garden is fun. Mom shows me how to pick the pumpkins, zucchini, and tomatoes. Then we plant seeds for carrots, lettuce, spinach, beets, and broccoli. I tell her about my robot race car, and she helps me practice my lines. Magnus follows me around and watches me work.

By Thursday I have nineteen dollars in my race car jar.

I don't know my lines by heart yet, but Ms. Anderson says we can read from our scripts at the first rehearsal tomorrow.

After dinner I take a break and practice my computer programming. I can't wait to get that race car robot and make it go.

It's not bedtime yet, so I ask Amanda to play a video game with me.

"Can't," she says. "More homework."

I try a few rounds of the video game by myself. But, it's not that much fun to play alone.

Then it's time for bed. I try to think about video games and race cars as I fall asleep, and *not* think about tomorrow's rehearsal.

The next day after lunch all the fourth graders go to the Multipurpose Room.

"Wow," I tell Adam, when I see the backdrop. "How did you make it look like stones?"

"I used a big sponge, and dipped it into paint," says Adam. "And stamped it here and there. Pretty cool, huh?"

"Super-cool," I say.

"Nice," says Nellie.

"Like a real castle," says Estella.

"Let's start at the beginning," says Ms. Anderson.

We're seated at lunch tables. Mr. Meaney stands behind us.

"Everyone who's in the first act, come up," says Ms. Anderson.

Nellie, Estella, and I climb the staircase on one side

of the stage. "Look," says Estella as we're going up. She points to a big box of white cloth on the floor in front of the stage. It's labeled COSTUMES. "I hope we're getting our toga fabric today."

Brittany and Ashley come up, along with 10 other kids who are servants and royal advisors.

"Go ahead, Nellie," says Mr. Meaney. "Read from the script if you don't know your lines yet."

Nellie opens her folder and begins. "Many years ago, in ancient Greece, there lived a king who loved gold."

This is where I'm supposed to walk out to my royal counting house. Right now it's just a lunch table that Adam and some other kids set up. There's a box on top, full of fake gold.

I walk out, open my folder, and read my first lines. "Gold, gold, gold! How I love gold."

"A little louder, Jake," says Ms. Anderson. She's standing at the front of the stage. She wears dangly earrings that match the seasons. Today they're snowflakes.

They swing as she walks across to the other side. "I'm sure you can remember that line now," she says. "Say it again. Look up at the audience and project your voice."

I look up and see Mr. Meaney and the other fourth graders watching me. Mr. Meaney holds up a hand and says, "I need to hear you from out here. Don't look at the microphone, but talk toward it."

Reading from my folder isn't so bad. But looking up and saying stuff to a bunch of people in the Multipurpose Room is nerve-wracking. Where is the mic?

"Go ahead," says Ms. Anderson.

I spot the mic and move toward it. "I sure do love gold. Gold, gold, gold." The mic makes a loud, cracking sound. Everyone laughs. My face feels hot.

"Good try, Jake!" Adam calls to me from the side of the stage.

"Better," says Mr. Meaney. "Don't worry about the mic. We'll get it adjusted."

They're all being nice but it's just making me nervous.

"Not quite so close to the mic this time, Jake. Pick up a handful of gold coins as you talk," says Ms. Anderson. "Show us you love gold."

"One more time," Ms. Anderson smiles at me.

My hands are sweaty. I forget my line and have to look at my folder.

I dig one hand into the box and scoop up some coins. "Gold, gold, gold. How I love gold." When I turn toward the mic, half of the coins fall out of my hand and onto the stage. One rolls on its edge to the front of the stage, spins around, and drops off. Everyone laughs.

"Let's move on," says Ms. Anderson. "Where are the princesses?"

Estella, Brittany, and Ashley come onstage as I pick up the gold.

"Go ahead, girls," says Ms. Anderson.

Brittany and Ashley open their folders.

Estella knows her line. She smiles and steps toward me. "Father, it is time for our royal breakfast."

"Perfect," says Mr. Meaney. "Good projecting, Estella."

Estella smiles and curtsies. The kids clap.

Brittany and Ashley step up, next to Estella.

"It's okay to read," says Ms. Anderson.

Ashley reads, "The royal cook is bringing golden apples, golden eggs, and golden raisin bread."

"Aren't you tired of gold food, Father?" I read. I hold my head up and try to project my voice.

The kids laugh.

"That's okay, Jake. You read Brittany's line. You'll get it." Ms. Anderson gives me a thumbs-up.

This is hard. It's hot with the stage lights on. I hope we're almost done. I wish I were in computer lab right now.

"Step toward the front of the stage while Brittany speaks," says Ms. Anderson. "You don't want to stand in front of her. Make sure the audience can see and hear her."

Brittany and I are facing each other, with our sides to the audience. I step sideways toward the front of the stage.

I'm looking at Brittany to see if I'm blocking her.

Brittany looks up from her folder and smiles at me. I hope I don't look as sweaty as I feel. I push my glasses up on my nose. Just to make sure I'm not blocking her, I take one more sideways step.

That's when I fall off the stage and land right in the middle of the costume box.

Chapter 6

Human Nature

"That could have happened to anybody," says Adam as we walk home.

"It wasn't that bad," says Estella.

"It was a graceful fall," says Nellie.

"I don't want to talk about it," I say.

Nellie insists. "We need another Worry Warrior's meeting. I'm nervous but I think you're even more jittery, Jake."

"Can we please stop talking about it? I just want to go home, walk Magnus, and play around on my computer."

"Nellie's right," says Estella. "You'll feel better if you talk about it."

"After the meeting, we can kick the soccer ball around," says Adam. "That always makes me feel better."

"You know what?" says Nellie. "We can have meetings every day after school. We'll practice our lines so much that it will be impossible for us to goof up."

"Really?" I say. "What about Magnus and Mrs. Jensen? And homework?"

"And soccer?" asks Adam.

"And ballet?" asks Estella.

"Just for half an hour," says Nellie. "Come straight home from school with me. You'll still be done in time for your other stuff."

"I guess that would be okay," I say. "Now that we've had our first rehearsal, I can see I need a lot of practice."

"Tomorrow's Saturday," Nellie says. "Can you guys do a kick-off meeting in the morning?"

We all agree to meet at Nellie's the next day.

Mrs. Jensen lets me bring Magnus to Nellie's house for

our meeting. He lies on a beanbag chair with his head on his paws and watches us. When we raise our hands and say "Don't worry, be happy!" his tail wags.

Nellie starts. "I didn't know it was going to be so scary up on stage."

"I know," I say. "Remember last year's show? The Multipurpose Room looked so big and far away. It was super-hot onstage. And with the lights in my eyes, it was hard to see the audience. I felt like a million strangers were staring at me. But at least last year, they were staring at *all* of us. Not just at me."

"When we had our dance recital last month, I wasn't nervous at practice," says Estella. "But on the night of the performance, I was scared. I told my mom I changed my mind and didn't want to do it."

"What happened?" asks Adam.

"My teacher showed me how to breathe," Estella puts her hand on her stomach and sucks in air. "And then relax my muscles like cooked noodles." She slumps over like a rag doll.

It looks pretty silly. "That helps?" I ask.

"It does," says Estella. "Also, she told me to focus on doing a good job, not on the audience. She said to pretend I'm doing a perfect rehearsal."

Adam says, "When I had to give that oral report last year, I was scared. You guys know I have trouble reading out loud. I memorized the report by listening to a recording, and then when I practiced giving the report, my mom made a video of me."

"Did that help?" I ask.

"Yes, it helped a lot," says Adam. "Want to try it? Since I don't have lines to learn, I could be the cameraman for you guys. I can use my tablet."

"Okay," says Nellie. "Let's read through our lines now. Monday we can try out our new ideas."

Adam and Magnus watch while we read our parts.

"You're good readers," says Adam. "But you look at your folders a lot."

"We need to learn our lines," says Nellie.

"I wonder if Ms. Anderson would let me tape X's on the stage to show you where to stand, Jake?" asks Adam.

"Great idea!" I say.

Estella says, "Jake and I need to get into character. We need to *be* Princess Marigold and King Midas."

"How do we do that?" I ask.

"Pretend you're King Midas. *Be* King Midas."

I put my finger on Adam's arm. "You're gold," I say. "Hey, now I can trade you in for cash and get my remote-control race car."

"Huh?" says Adam.

"Didn't you read the myth?" asks Nellie.

"I'm not in the play," he says.

"You're still supposed to read it," says Estella.

"I am?" Adam's pocket timer dings. "Saved by the bell," he laughs. "Soccer practice."

We adjourn the meeting and Magnus and I walk Adam to practice.

"Want to hear the story of King Midas?" I ask.

"Sure," says Adam.

"So, there's this king," I begin. "He loves gold more than anything. One day he finds a satyr—that's someone who is half goat, half man—in his rose garden. Midas is nice to the satyr, who turns out to be a friend of the god Dionysius. Dionysius wants to thank Midas for being kind to his friend. He gives him one wish."

"Cool," says Adam.

"King Midas's wish is to turn everything he touches into gold," I say. "But now he can't eat, because his food turns to gold. Worst of all, he accidentally turns his daughters to gold."

"Wow," says Adam.

"King Midas realizes he made a big mistake. He can't eat. He misses his daughters. He begs Dionysius to take away the wish."

"He should have said that wish differently," says Adam. "He should have just asked for a giant crate of gold."

"Yeah," I say. "But I think the point is more about human nature. King Midas was greedy. When he got his wish, he learned that his daughters were more important to him than gold."

"I guess," says Adam. "Still, we should think about what to wish for if we ever get the chance. So we don't goof it up like he did."

I think about the $19 in my money jar. Today is allowance day, so when I add nine dollars I'll have $28. It's going to take another five weeks to earn enough for a robot race car. I wish Dionysius would give me a wish. Five minutes of Midas touch would come in handy right now.

Chapter 7

Beach Street Hobbies

I wake up on Sunday morning to the smell of bacon. That means Mom is making eggs and pancakes too. I grab my King Midas folder and go into the kitchen.

Mom is scrambling eggs. Six blueberry pancakes are on the griddle, ready to be flipped.

Amanda is sitting at the kitchen table looking at cupcake-making ideas on the laptop.

"Want to help me practice my lines?" I ask her.

"No," she snaps, without looking up.

"You don't have to be rude," I snap back. Last year, Amanda helped me practice my Winter Extravaganza songs a lot. Why is she so grumpy now?

I plop down, open my folder, and read my first lines. Then I try to say them without looking.

"How I love gold. Gold, gold, gold." After that, I'm stuck.

"Can you do that somewhere else?" asks Amanda. "I'm trying to concentrate."

"On cupcake decorations?" I say. "Who cares what a cupcake looks like if it tastes good?"

"Lots of people!" says Amanda. "What are you talking about? What's wrong with you?"

I know it was a mean thing to say, but Amanda started it. I blurt out, "You're always complaining that you have too much homework to help me with my lines or play video games like we used to, but you have plenty of time to decorate stupid cupcakes!"

"For your information," says Amanda, "Lucy and I are going to start a cupcake business. Cupcakes are just as important as your stupid robot race car! Cupcakes are an art form. They make people happy!"

"Hey," says Mom as she puts butter, syrup, and orange juice on the table. "What's going on with you two? It's not like you to argue."

"Ask Amanda," I say. "She started it."

"Did not," says Amanda.

"Who started it doesn't matter. Stop it now," says Mom.

Amanda and I frown at each other as we eat.

"How's it going with the play?" Mom asks.

I'm glad for a change of subject. "If I had my lines on cards," I say, "it would make it easier to carry them around and practice."

"Why not type them into the computer after breakfast?" suggests Mom. "We can print them onto card stock."

"Good idea!" I say.

Once the dishes are done I get to work. It's a lot of lines, but we learned keyboarding in computer lab in second and third grade, so I'm pretty fast. I find that typing the words helps me learn them.

Mom has card stock for the printer. She helps me format my document so we can print it out and trim it to index-card size with her paper cutter.

Then I have the idea of punching a hole in the corner of each card to hold them together with a ring. But we don't have any rings.

Mom says, "Let's walk downtown and get some at Beach Street Hobbies. They have school supplies."

"I need a notebook for English, too," Amanda says to Mom. She isn't looking at me.

We put on our shoes and head downtown.

Beach Street is a busy place on Sunday morning. People are sitting at sidewalk cafés drinking coffee and reading newspapers. Dog walkers are crossing at the signal to go to the big park in the center of town. Moms and dads are pushing babies in strollers.

"What do you want for your birthday dinner next weekend?" Mom asks Amanda. "Should we invite Lucy?"

"Yes," Amanda says. "I'd love that."

I forgot it was almost Amanda's birthday. Mom lets us choose our birthday dinner every year.

"Let's have spaghetti and salad," says Amanda. "And lemon blueberry cupcakes."

"Yum!" Mom says.

I don't say anything. If Amanda's still mad at me then I'm still mad at her.

***

Beach Street Hobbies is stocked for the holidays. The store is huge, and the front aisles are covered with decorations. It smells like cinnamon and cloves. We walk past the ornaments, jingle bells, and snowmen. Then we go past aisles of colorful yarn and knitting needles. When we reach the school supplies, Amanda picks a notebook. I find four metal rings for my cards.

"Oh, look, Mom!" Amanda points to the next section. It's filled with cake-decorating equipment. There are brightly colored cupcake liners, muffin tins, mixers, icing kits, and cookbooks.

"When Lucy and I start our cupcake business, we're going to get all of this stuff."

The next aisle is covered with fake flowers and leaves. I think of my costume. "Mom, Ms. Anderson gave me the cloth for my toga. But I need to make a leaf crown."

"Those are called laurel wreathes," says Mom. "We'll need a headband and some of these leaves."

"Also, I'm supposed to have a gold belt and sandals," I add.

"Let's get gold ribbon while we're here," says Mom. "We'll use some for a belt, and glue some to your flip-flops."

After we find everything, Mom pays for our supplies and we leave.

"I wish I didn't have to wear this costume," I tell Mom, as we walk back down Beach Street.

"What bothers you about it?" asks Mom.

"It's weird that it only goes over one shoulder," I say. "What if other kids laugh at me for wearing a dress?"

"They'll be wearing dresses, too, if they're in the play," says Mom.

"Good point," I say. "But what if it slips off? It's only tied at one shoulder."

"You can practice tying it tightly," says Mom. "I'll help you. Maybe I can sew in a snap or some Velcro."

"Can I wear jeans and a T-shirt underneath?" I ask.

"Amanda," says Mom, "do you remember how they did it when you were in fourth grade?"

I wonder if Amanda's going to answer. She still seems mad. But then she says, "No T-shirt. But the guys wore gym shorts underneath."

"Oh. Okay," I say. This is good information. At least if it slips off or falls apart, I won't be standing in the middle of the stage in my underwear. Of course, standing in the middle of the stage in nothing but my gym shorts doesn't sound that great, either.

Chapter 8

Dress Rehearsal

The next week we practice every day after school in the Worry Warrior's clubhouse. Adam uses the video camera in his tablet to record us. It helps a lot. When I watch a recording of myself, I notice things. Like, that I'm not looking up. Or that I sound like I'm reading. We talk about it. Then we practice again and make it better.

By Thursday I can say most of my lines by heart. Estella says I sound more like King Midas and less like Jake.

Mom likes to sing, so while we make dinner or work in the garden, she helps me practice the song at the end of the play. It's called "The Best Things in Life Are Free." The good news is, everybody has to sing, not just King Midas.

I now have $43 in my jar. All that dog walking and vegetable gardening is fun, but it still feels like it's taking a long time to earn enough money for my robot race car.

I'm glad Mrs. Jensen's ankle is getting better. I can tell she doesn't like sitting around. I think she's almost as excited about the race car as I am. I bring our laptop over and show her how I can write programs to control the car. With my allowance and the extra money, I should have enough in four more weeks. I practice my programming whenever I can, so I'll be ready.

Friday after lunch is dress rehearsal. Ms. Anderson says, "One more week until the Winter Extravaganza. Today you're going to wear your costumes and do the play as if it's the night of the performance. No stopping, or talking, or asking for help. Are we ready?"

Some kids mumble and groan. Nellie, Estella, Adam, and I look at each other and do a thumbs-up.

"I feel good about this," Nellie says when we're standing with Estella offstage.

We tie our toga fabric over our school clothes. It looks silly, if you ask me. And it keeps opening up on the sides. My costume definitely needs more work before next Friday.

Brittany, Ashley, and the other kids are on the opposite side of the stage.

Adam is over there, too. He's standing next to Ms. Anderson. She signals Nellie to get ready. The royal advisors and servants find their places.

When everyone is settled, Nellie walks out in front of the closed curtain. I hear her say her line perfectly. "Many years ago, in ancient Greece, there lived a king who loved gold."

Then Adam pulls the cord to open the curtain.

I walk out to the middle of the stage and stand next to the table. "Gold, gold, gold. How I love gold," I say. So far, so good. The mic doesn't boom or crackle, and I remember my line. I look out at the audience. I even scoop up a few coins without dropping them.

The princesses come out and say their lines. Brittany

has a pretty gold clasp holding her toga at the shoulder. She looks like a real Greek princess. I feel myself starting to blush. I think of robots to calm down.

The play continues. The stage lights feel hotter and hotter. Wearing my toga over my school clothes does not help.

Still, things go well. I remember my lines while I am at breakfast with my princess daughters.

We go offstage, the curtain closes, and Adam and his team change the backdrop. Now we're in the castle rose garden.

I go out, find the satyr, and invite him to stay at the castle. Dionysius shows up and grants my wish.

One more change of backdrops and I'm back inside the castle. I realize I can't eat anything. My food turns to gold when I touch it. Then comes the big scene, where I turn my daughters to gold.

Estella, Brittany, and Ashley skip across the stage, do a ballet twirl, and hold out their hands to me.

"Hello, Father," they say.

I touch their hands and they freeze. It's pretty awesome. They honestly look like statues.

"Oh, my daughters!" I say. "What have I done?"

I touch Estella, Ashley, and Brittany on the head.

"I've turned my daughters to gold. Oh no!" I cry out.

Estella and Ashley are staring straight ahead, not moving a muscle. But Brittany moves her eyes and looks at me. I push my glasses up on the bridge of my nose. Why is it so hot up here? Now I've forgotten my next line.

I look to the side of the stage for Ms. Anderson's cue card. Where is she? I take a small step and twist around to look at the other side. Oops, I bump into a chair and lose my balance.

I grab the first thing I can—the curtain. At first it feels solid and I tighten my grip on the velvet fabric. Then I hear a ripping sound. I feel myself falling. The harder I grip, the more ripping I hear. As the ripping stops, my feet slip out from under me and I land on my back on the hard wood

stage. The curtain must have ripped completely, because it lands on top of me. I'm lying on my back on the floor of the stage, covered by the ripped curtain.

I hear the kids in the Multipurpose Room laughing. I hear the kids onstage laughing. I can't hear them, but I wouldn't be surprised if Ms. Anderson and Mr. Meaney were laughing, too.

I imagine what I look like: a big lump of ripped, red velvet. I'm not hurt, but I sure feel bad. I think I'll just stay under this curtain and never come out.

Chapter 9

Time Flies When You're Having Fun

Saturday morning Mom is busy in the kitchen when I get up.

"Hi Jake!" she says, cheerfully. She's pulling flour and sugar from the cupboard.

I pour myself a bowl of cereal. "What are you making?" I ask.

"Amanda's cupcakes," she replies. "Want to help?"

"Sure! Where's Amanda?" I pour milk and grab a spoon.

"She had to leave early for a cheerleader carwash," Mom says.

"Is Lucy coming tonight?" I ask.

"Yes," mom answers. "I invited the whole family. Want to help me make a big pot of spaghetti sauce?"

"Sure." Mom, Amanda, and I have always had fun cooking together. There's a TV cooking show we like. This goofy guy tells the science and history behind the food he cooks. Sometimes we try his recipes.

Now I pull up his website and get the recipe for spaghetti with meat sauce. Mom and I read it over.

"We'll need to go to the grocery store," says Mom. "And I need decorations at Beach Street Hobbies."

I go to my room to put my shoes on, and think about what to give Amanda. When we were little, we made each other cards. Last year she was into this series of books about cheerleaders, and I got her the latest book. This year she wants a cell phone, but that's too expensive. She likes new clothes, but I don't know how to pick those. I guess I'll bring my money and look around at Beach Street Hobbies.

Mom drives us to the grocery store and we get what we

need. Then we go to Beach Street Hobbies and Mom picks out some decorations.

I see the cupcake-making stuff and remember how much Amanda liked it when we were there before. There's a set of icing tips that make different shapes. They're stainless steel. There are 25 different tips. They screw onto a pastry bag that you fill with icing. It's like the one they use on Amanda's favorite TV cupcake show.

The kit is $39.95. That's a lot. There's tax, too. If I get it, I'll have to wait another couple of weeks for my race car. And that's if Mrs. Jensen still needs me to work for her.

I'm trying to decide what to do when Mom comes down the aisle. "Find something?" she asks.

"I think Amanda would like this," I say.

"That's really nice," says Mom.

"It's a lot of money," I say. "But I have that much saved up so I can afford it."

"It is a lot to spend," says Mom. "Amanda would really like it. But you've been working hard to earn money for your race car, too. Are you really ok with spending it all?"

"What do you think I should do?" I ask.

"You have to be the one to decide," says Mom. "We can look around some more if you'd like."

Even though I'm still sort of mad at her, I think Amanda is an awesome sister. If she wants to start a cupcake business with Lucy, I want her to have the right tools.

"I'm going to get it," I say.

"You're sure?" asks Mom.

"I'm sure," I say.

By the time we get home, Mom and I are starving. We eat leftover pizza for lunch and then get to work on the spaghetti sauce.

Next, Mom helps me wrap my gift, and then I go to check on Mrs. Jensen and Magnus.

"Jake, I'm glad to see you," says Mrs. Jensen. She's got her foot propped up again. "I think I overdid it yesterday.

I was hoping you could walk Magnus today."

"Sure," I tell Mrs. Jensen. "I'm sorry you're still having trouble with your ankle."

"Thanks, Jake. I'll survive! More importantly, how's the play going?" she asks as I snap on Magnus's leash.

I tell her about the big goof-up yesterday.

"That's what dress rehearsals are for," she says. "You make your mistakes then, so it will go smoothly at the real performance."

"I never thought of it that way," I say. I feel better. Maybe I've already made all of the mistakes there are to make. That would be awesome.

Amanda is home when I get back. She and Mom are decorating the cupcakes.

"Do you want help practicing your lines when we're done here?" asks Mom.

"I know my lines, but I'm worried about my toga," I tell her.

Amanda surprises me by saying, "I'll help you fix it so it won't fall off."

"Really?" I say.

"Sure," she says, as if we never had a fight.

I bring my supplies out and tie the cloth on over my gym shorts. Amanda fixes the knot on one shoulder so it's tight. Then she uses safety pins to close the open sides. Now it feels really solid. I'm not worried about it falling off.

"What do you think?" I ask her.

"Looks like a dress," she says.

We both laugh.

"Hey, Amanda," I say. "I'm sorry I said your cupcakes are stupid."

"Yeah," she says. "I'm sorry I'm always so busy."

"I guess that's how it is when you get to middle school," I say.

"Well," says Amanda. "You'll have an easier time of it when you get to sixth grade. You're good at school."

"Really?" I say. "It seems like you're good at everything."

"Schoolwork is harder for me," she says. "Especially math."

"I'm sorry you didn't get to be the lead in your Greek play. You would have been way better at it than me," I say.

Amanda smiles and bumps my arm with her elbow. "You'll be great," she says.

I elbow-bump her back. It helps that my sister thinks I'll do well.

Next, we glue the leaves to the headband to make a laurel wreath. We glue gold ribbon onto my flip-flops, and add gold strings that go over my ankles in a criss-cross.

"Awesome," says Amanda when I have my entire costume on. "How does it feel?"

"Embarrassing," I say, as I unplug the glue gun. "But I don't think it'll fall off. Thanks again for your help!"

I feel better about my costume. But I'm glad it's time to take it off and get ready for Amanda's birthday dinner.

I blow up balloons and hang the Happy Birthday banner while Amanda sets the table and Mom makes a salad. The doorbell rings, and Nellie's family is here.

I show Nellie's dad and big brother, Henry, the website for my robot car. They agree, it's going to be awesome!

"This spaghetti is good!" says Lucy to Mom after we all sit down and start dinner.

"Jake helped," says Mom.

Lucy gives me a thumbs-up.

Henry eats two big helpings, so I know he likes it.

Then it's time for dessert. Mom arranges 12 cupcakes on a fancy plate. Each one has a candle in the center. She lights them and we sing "Happy Birthday" to Amanda. She takes a deep breath and blows them out.

Next, it's time to open presents. Amanda unwraps mine last. Her eyes open wide when she sees the decorating kit.

"You got that for me, Jake?" she says. "Lucy, look at all these tips!

"It's amazing!" Lucy smiles.

"Thank you, Jake!" Amanda gives me a big hug. "What about your race car?" she asks.

"I'll still get it," I tell her. "It'll just take a little longer."

"That's so sweet," she says. "I know you've been working really hard to save."

She hugs me, and I feel like I made the right choice. "It'll go by fast," I gulp.

Time flies when you're having fun, I think. At least I sure hope so.

Chapter 10

The Best Things in Life Are Free

It's the Friday night before winter break. The third graders have just finished their performance. We had to wait in our classroom while they sang. Now we come in through the backstage side door, so the audience can't see us.

I've got my toga on over my gym shorts. The knot is tied tightly. Both sides are closed with as many safety pins as Mom and Amanda could fit. I'm wearing my gold belt and sandals.

Nellie, Estella, Brittany, and Ashley are wearing makeup. Their cheeks are rosy, their lips are glossy, and their hair is shiny.

We have silly laurel wreathes around our heads. Actually, the girls' wreathes look pretty.

My hands are sweaty. My stomach feels jumpy. I couldn't eat my dinner. I'm not sure I remember any of my lines. My glasses keep sliding down the bridge of my nose and I have to push them back up. I never noticed how much I do this until Adam videotaped us practicing.

Nellie is jiggling her arms and switching her weight from one leg to the other.

"Take a deep breath," Estella tells us both.

Nellie and I breathe in and out.

"I think I'm going to be sick," says Nellie.

Me, too, I want to say. But I don't want to say that in front of Brittany.

Brittany shakes out her arms and then her legs. "I'm feeling nervous too."

Now I'm worried about Brittany. I don't want her to feel nervous. "You look nice," I tell her.

She smiles and says, "You too. Like Hercules Jones."

"Really?" I say, amazed. Hercules Jones is this awesome character in a series of books that we've all read. He has dyslexia, like Adam. He finds out his ancestors are Greek gods. He has superpowers. He's cool. Brittany thinks I look like him? I try not to blush.

Ms. Anderson is waving her cue cards on the other side of the stage. Adam makes the lights backstage blink on and off. That means it's time to start.

The lights in the Multipurpose Room go dim, and the lights onstage go bright. The kids take their places. Ms. Anderson motions for Nellie to start.

I hear Nellie give her introduction. It sounds perfect. The audience gives her a big round of applause.

Then the curtain goes slowly, painfully, up.

I'm supposed to walk out. My legs don't want to do it.

Walk, legs. You're King Midas. You can do it.

I take a deep breath. I walk onstage. I look out at a gazillion faces. The lights are shining right in my eyes.

The Multipurpose Room is dark. The audience is huge. Where is my family?

I take a deep breath. Out of the corner of my eye, I see Ms. Anderson holding up my cue card. I'm supposed to start. Now.

I take one more breath. Adam is standing next to Ms. Anderson. He smiles and does a Worry Warrior hand signal.

I can do this. I'm like Hercules Jones. I think about all the millions of times we practiced our lines. And Adam videotaped us. I think about how Mom helped me learn my song, and Amanda helped me with my costume.

I scoop up a handful of gold pieces and look right out at the audience. "Gold, gold gold," I say. My voice is loud and clear. I'm projecting. "How I love gold."

Estella dances out with Ashley and Brittany. We all remember our lines. I don't drop anything, or fall off the stage, or knock anything over.

I think I might have done all right. I sure hope so.

After my eyes adjust, I find Mom and Amanda in the audience. They brought Mrs. Jensen, too.

I'm having fun! The audience watches intently. They laugh at the funny parts, and they look worried at the sad parts.

When we reach the end, we all stand together and sing "The Best Things in Life Are Free." The crowd goes wild. We get a standing ovation. It's the best school play ever.

ABOUT THE AUTHOR

Marne Ventura is the author of 29 children's books, 10 of them for Capstone. A former elementary school teacher, she holds a master's degree in education from the University of California. When she's not writing, she enjoys arts and crafts, cooking and baking, and spending time with her family. Marne lives with her husband on the central coast of California. This is her first venture into fiction.

ABOUT THE ILLUSTRATOR

Leo Trinidad is an illustrator and animator who has created many animated characters and television shows for companies including Disney and Dreamworks, but his great passion is illustrating children's books. Leo graduated with honors from the Veritas University of Arts and Design in San Jose, Costa Rica, where he lives with his wife and daughter. Visit him online at www.leotrinidad.com

GLOSSARY

astrophysicist—a scientist who studies objects in space such as planets, stars, and moons

clove—a spice used in cooking

dyslexia—a learning disability that is usually marked by problems in reading, spelling, and writing

electronics—products that run on small amounts of electricity, including laptops, smart phones, and TVs

eucalyptus—a fragrant evergreen tree that grows in dry climates

mythology—old or ancient stories told again and again that help connect people with the past

narrator—a person who tells a story or describes an event

programmer—a person who writes instructions to make a computer work a certain way

project—to make your voice carry very far

satyr—a creature in Greek mythology with a face and body like a human and ears, legs, and tail like a goat

videotape—to record both the picture and sound

Viking—a group of Scandinavian warriors who raided Europe in the 8th to 10th centuries

TALK ABOUT IT

1. Jake was really nervous about having such a big part in the school play, so he talked to his friends about his worries. What else might he have done?

2. Jake admits that he misses his sister now that she is in middle school. Talk about how you've felt when a sibling or friend moved away.

3. Jake really wanted a robot car more than anything in the world. Has there ever been anything you wanted that much? What did you do to try to get it?

WRITE ABOUT IT

1. Think about a time you were worried about something. Write about how you felt and what you did to feel better.

2. Who is your favorite character in this story? Draw a picture of that person. Then write a list of five things you like about him or her.

3. How would you have helped Jake with his worry? Think about that, and then write down what you would have done.

Worry WARRIORS

Nervous Nellie
Fights First-day Frenzy

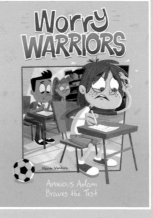

Anxious Adam
Braves the Test

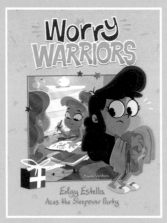

Edgy Estella
Aces the Sleepover Party

Jittery Jake
Conquers Stage Fright